SUPERWORLD

A DIFFERENT WORLD FROM REALITY

SONIA MARANDI

I want to thank myself because I promised myself to complete this book before my birthday. So this book is also a birthday gift for me. And, thanks to the editor for editing this book and thanks to everyone who is going to read this book or read this book already. Thank you, everyone...

Contents

Foreword

My goal is to entertain you all and show my creativity by writing books. Many people like other types of stories but I like Thriller, suspicious, crime stories. There are many stories I think I didn't know how to show to people so, I wrote stories which I like! and I hope you like my stories.

Preface

I had already wrote this story when I was 10, I again read the story, it was intresting but it needed some changes so I thought to change it and write this book. While I was writing this book, I was very intrested in quirks, super powers. So, I added quirks, and some fights. But, my previous version of this story didn't had any crime stories, so I added them. I really liked my old story, so I made this. And, I am very happy to know about my old stories.

Acknowledgements

Message from the author: I want to thank those who have helped in making my book! special thanks to the editor, she has helped me so much! she made all this for you. And again I want to thank them so much for helping me in making this book. Not to forget my viewers who read and view my books...

Prologue

Anita Hemishan, is the protoganist of the story. She came to a new town called Super Town, and met new people. Later, on her high school a mysterious child attacked many children, he was known as the strange guy. So, Anita started to know about him, she wanted to solve the mystery...

CHAPTER I

Introduction

Superworld, a world in which people have superpowers known as Quirk. Quirks are based on elements and power personalities. Examples of elements are Electric, Fire, Water, Air, Ice, Rock, Earth, Sand, etc. Quirk is related to Elements and Power Personality, An quirk example; elements is earth and power personality is healer, can heal people with flowers and summon different types of flowers. There are 5 power personalities; Sneaker/ Sneak Attacker- 20% of people are sneaker/ sneak attackers. Sneaker, which always sneaks or hides, sneak attacker, which sneaks and then attacks. Sneaker and Sneak Attacker come in the same category. Defender- 20%, Defender, which defend themselves or their team from enemies. Tricker- 20%, Tricker which tricks, confuse the enemy. Attacker- 30%, Attacker, who directly attacks the enemy. Healer-10%, Healer, which heals people. People have two quirks, The main and the Branch, The main quirk will be always with them. The branch quirk's purpose is to help the person, if in a situation the main quirk is not helpful so they can use their branch quirk, but at the age of 40, they will lose their branch quirk. They will get these quirks from their parents. Quirks have tiers and levels also! In each tier they will get a new ability of their quirk, there are 5 tiers, Low Tier [lvl 1.0-1.9], Mid Tier [lvl 2.0- 3.4], Elite Tier [lvl 3.5-4.9], High Tier [lvl 5.0+], God tier [6.0+]. For example, the low tier (1.4) can heal people in 1 minute, in the Mid Tier (2.9), the time goes to 30 seconds. About Superworld; The protagonist, Anita Hemishan lives in the country named,

Wendon. In the town, Super Town. Their currency is Qoin (Q), and Superqoin (SQ). But, all the countries hate each other and sometimes war will also start, that's why no one is allowed to go to other countries.

CHAPTER II

1st day in Super Town

Anita Hemishan, a normal 17-year-old student, studies in S.P (Superpower) High School, Wendon. Anita was from Claytown, she was transferred to Super Town. It was her first day of high school, and she was very excited, "Mom! Today I will meet new people and make new friends!" She said to her mom, "Yes Crete" Her mom said. (Crete is Anita's nickname.) "At Claytown, no one talked to me, I hope I will make some friends," Anita said. And she went to High School. Anita went to her classroom and sat on a bench, a few minutes later, the teacher came, she said, "Children, today we have a new student and her name is Anita Hemishan, so, Anita come here and introduce yourself", Anita went near the teacher and said, "Hello! I am Anita, and I have come from Claytown, I hope you all become my friends". Someone asked "What about your quirks?" Anita became nervous, "Yes! Tell your quirks also," The teacher said, "M-My quirk is that I can summon walls and invisible anything", everyone started to laugh, "What a loser... so you are a defender and a sneaker?!" Someone asked, "Yes" Anita replied, and students laughed more, Anita felt very sad, "Please don't laugh, you should not laugh at someone!" The teacher said, but everyone ignored her. Anita became sad, and after school, she went home. "So, how was your day?" Her mom asked, "Not good" Anita replied, "What? You didn't make any friends?" Her mom asked, "Yes... No one talked to me... And everyone made fun of me because I am a defender and a sneaker!" Anita said in a sad tone, "Don't worry crete, ignore them, let them talk whatever they want! Just ignore and be happy for being such unique! And, about making friends, maybe tomorrow you will" Her mother cheered her, "thanks mom for cheering me, Mom can I go outside at 5 PM?" Anita asked, "Sure! Now go and wash your face and rest a little," Her mom said. Anita went to her room.

About Anita Hemishan-

Anita's nickname is Crete, born on 20th May 2004, a 17-year-old student, her quirk; Main- Can make walls at any height, (Right now, can only do till 1 meter). Element; Sand. Power Personality; Defender. Got the quirk from her father. Branch- make anything invisible (Right now, can invisible herself and change the transparency of the items). Element; Air. Power Personality; Sneaker. Got the quirk from her mother. Level; 2.7 (Mid Tier). Has blue eyes and blonde hair. The story about her nickname; Her Mother thought Anita makes walls of Concrete, so she started to call her Con, but Anita didn't like it so her mother started to call her Crete, and that's how she got the nickname. Anita also has a wound on her neck because, when she was young and learning how to control quirks, she hurt herself and so she got the wound. Anita also wears a heart-shaped necklace. One side is blue color which represents her mother as she has blue eyes and the other side is the golden color representing her father as he has golden eyes. This is the tradition of Hemishan, every generation has to wear a heart-shaped necklace until they get married because, after marriage, they have to wear a round-shaped necklace with their eye color to represent themselves.

Anita lay down in her bed, and thought something, "I have the most useless quirk a person can ever have! A quirk which can defend themselves?!" Anita didn't like her quirks. At 5 PM, Anita's mother called her, "Crete! You were going to go outside now, right? C'mon, be ready and let's go!" She said, Anita got ready and they went outside... They went to the park and saw a place called 'Duel and Duel Practice' Anita got excited by seeing it, and asked her mother, "Mother! Can I go there?" "Sure Crete, just be careful!" Anita's mother said, "Okay mom!" Anita said and went towards that place, she saw a man, having bright blue hair and dull dark eyes. Anita told the man, "Good evening! I have come to do a duel" "Sure child, what's your name and level?" "My name is Anita Hemishan and my level is 2.7" "Okay... As you are a Mid Tier, you are allowed to do duels! Now, let me introduce you to myself. I am Darrel Powell and I teach children to duel and let them duel each other! I am also sure if children didn't get that much hurt by duel" Darrel said, "Okay Sir. And thank you for the permission" Anita said, "But... You can't duel here for free. You have to give 10sq (superqoin- Wendon's currency)" Darrel said, "Okay sir..." Anita replied and gave him 10sq. Darrel looked toward a bunch of children and shouted, "Who is willing to do a duel? They can raise their hand" Darrel said, A girl with purple hair raised her hand, "Oh... Daisy..." Darrel said, "Daisy?" Anita thought, "Sir, I am willing to do a duel!" Daisy said, Anita saw her, she had shiny black eyes. "But Daisy! Are you okay to fight with your healing quirks?" Darrel asked, "Yes Sir, everyone should know some sort of defending or attacking tricks, even though they have healing or sneaking quirks!" Daisy said, "If it's okay for then, okay! Now before this duel, you both have to give your introduction" Darrel said, Daisy went towards Anita, raised her hand and handshakes her, and introduced herself to Anita, "My name is Anupma Reshan, my main quirk is that I can summon any type of flowers and with that, I can heal anyone. So it is an Earth element and a healer.

Now, can you tell me your quirks?" Anupma said, "My main quirk is that I can create walls made out of materials like sand, concrete, etc. It is a sand element and a defender" Anita said, "My branch quirk is that I can travel in electric components. And it is an electric element and a sneaker. What about you?" Daisy said, "My branch quirk is that I can make anything invisible," Anita said, "Now! Start the duel!" Darrel shouted.

Anita invites herself, Anupma was confused but when she looked behind, she saw Anita with a rock made out of her wall, but before Anita could throw it at Anupma, she disappeared, Anupma traveled on the switchboard, "Huff! That was close" She thought. Anupma turned the tables. Anita looked behind and it was Anupma with a prickle of a rose plant, she was going to stab Anita with it, but before it could happen, Anita summoned a wall in front. But, Anupma came in front of Anita and threw the prickles, Anita was not able to defend herself, so she got prickles in her body and fell. Anupma was happy but not for long... A wall came in front of her, she looked behind and it was Anita with the same rock, Anupma panicked and was not able to defend herself, Anita threw the rock and summoned more rocks and threw them at Daisy. At last, Anupma said, "Ok stop! You win!" "Ok, I will stop," Anita said. And so, Anita won and Anupma lost. "Looks like Anita wins! Congratulations!" Darrel said, Anita was happy, she looked at Anupma, and she was hurt. So, Anita said, "Are you alright? Did I hurt you too much?" "I am fine!" Anupma said, and she summoned a flower (sunflower) and put it on her wounds, Anita was confused, but a few minutes later, Anupma was healed by her flowers! "Look! I am healed!" Anupma said, "Good to hear it" Anita replied, "You had given 10sq for the participation in the duel, you would get 100sq for winning the duel!" Darrel said, "Thank you, sir!" Anita said in a jolly tone. "And... Daisy! As I liked your strategy, here is your 50sq. I liked when you hid in the switchboard!" Darrel said, "Thank you, sir!" Anupma said. "Crete! Should I heal you?" Anupma asked, "Yes! Also, Daisy, I liked your strategy, so can we be friends?" Anita asked, "Sure! I will be your friend!" Anupma said, "Now, come! I will heal you!" Anupma said, Anita came closer to Anupma, Anupma summoned her flowers and put them in Anita's wounds. A few minutes later, Anita was healed! "Look! You are healed!", Anita tried to touch her wounds and it wasn't there! She was surprised, "Oh yes! Thank you, Daisy!" Anita said. Suddenly, a girl with red hair and green eyes and a boy with grey hair and indigo eyes were arguing. Anita saw them. "This is all your fault! Who takes this much time to get ready!? Are we going to a function or something?!" The boy said, "Who told you to be ready so early?!" The girl said, "Oh my god, they again started arguing!" Anupma said, "You two! Stop!" Anupma said in an annoyed voice, "Daisy... who are they?" Anita asked, The boy saw Anita and started to blush, "They are my cousins!" Anupma said, "Oh..." Anita replied, The girl notices the boy blushing, "Bro, why are you blushing?" The girl asked, "What are you even talking about?" The boy replied, "Well, I have to go!" The boy said and went away. "Are you thinking what I am thinking?" The girl said to Anupma, "Yes!" Anupma replied, "Uhh... What happened to me? Why I was blushing after seeing her?" The boy asked himself and came back. The girl and Anupma were teasing the boy and laughing. "Daisy, who is she?" The boy asked, "She is my new friend, Anita Hemishan, you can also call her Crete. Now, Crete, this is Daniel Wendon, also known as Rain and this is Mouny Reshan, also known as Plus.

"Hello~ Nice to meet you both!" Anita said, Daniel blushed and said with Mouny, "Hello! Nice to meet with you too!" "I have a question for Rain," Anita said, "What question?" Daniel asked, "I have noticed that, since we have met, you are blushing...why so?" Anita asked, "Oh~ Even I don't know what happened to me..." Daniel said and blushed. "So, why had we come here?" Mouny asked, "Oh my god! You again forgot!" Daniel said angrily, "Shut up!" Mouny replied angrily, "Guys! Before you both again argue! You have come here to duel each other!" Anupma said, "Oh yeah..." Mouny said with a grinning face. "Then let's go to Duel and Duel Practice," Daniel said and they went to that place, "Sir, we have come here to do a duel," Daniel said to Darrel, "You both will duel each other?" Darrel asked, "Yes sir!" Daniel and Mouny said, "That's not possible" Darrel replied, "But, why sir?" Mouny asked, "As you both know each other, so you both will also know each other's quirk! Then, this would be an unfair on-the-spot duel!" Darrel explained. "Now either you can duel with a

random person or can duel each other outside!" Darrel said, "Ok sir! We would go outside and duel each other" Daniel and Mouny said, "Okay" Darrel replied. And they went outside, "Now, both get ready!" Anupma said Daniel saw Anita sitting on a bench some distance away, "Crete! What are you doing here?" Daniel asked, "I thought to see your duel so I was waiting here," Anita said, "Oh~," Daniel said and blushed, "Are you guys ready?" Anupma asked, "Yes!" Daniel and Mouny said, "Start!" Anupma said. The duel has started...

Daniel and Mouny's quirks;-

Daniel Wendon, Quirks- Main; Control lighting strikes. Branch; Makes a fire sword. Elements- Main; Electric. Branch; Fire. Power Personality- Main; Attacker. Branch;

Attacker. Level; 2.6- Mid Tier.

Mouny Reshan, Quirks- Main; Spread fire at many distances and can control it. Branch; Summon anything made of ice. Elements- Main; Fire. Branch; Ice. Power Personality- Main; Attacker. Branch; Tricker. Level; 2.5- Mid Tier.

(More information is at the end of this chapter)

Mouny summoned her ice cubes and throws them, but Daniel made a fire sword and defended with it. And tries to summon a lightning strike, "He is summoning the lightning strike," Mouny thought, so she started to spread fire, the fire caught Daniel's leg and everyone was shocked. "Well, I don't care!" Daniel said, "What do you mean by that?" Mouny asked, she was going to throw more ice cubes until a bolt of lightning struck her, she was damaged a lot but didn't die. "Plus, do you accept the defeat?" Anupma asked, "Of course not!" Mouny said Daniel tried to attack Mouny with his fire sword, but, Mouny collapsed. After a few minutes, Mouny's eyes opened, "What happened to me?" She asked, "You collapsed! And Rain won the duel!" Anupma said. "Congratulations Rain!" Anita said to Daniel, "Thanks..." Daniel replied and blushed. He looked at the clock, "Look it's 7 PM! Let's go home!" He said, and they went to their house.

About Anupma Reshan:-

Anupma's nickname is Daisy. Born on 2nd September 2004, a 17-year-old student. Her quirks; Main- Can summon any type of flowers and heal anyone with that. (Right now, can heal within 1 minute). Element; Earth. Power Personality; Healer. Got the quirk from her mother. Branch- can travel in electric components. (Right now, can stay in the components for 10 minutes). Element; Electric. Power Personality; Sneaker. Got the quirk from her father.

Level, 2.5- Mid Tier. Has black eyes and purple hair. The short story about her nickname; When Anupma was a child, she tried to summon a flower and it was a daisy! She liked a flower and it became her favorite flower. Her cousins called her Daisy and so it became her nickname.

About Mouny Reshan:-

Mouny's nickname is Plus. Born on 27th January 2004, an 18-year-old student, Her quirks; Main- Spread Fire at many distances. (Right now, can spread it within 10 meters and 5 of them at once). Element; Fire. Power Personality; Attacker. Got the quirk from her father. Branch- summon anything made of ice. (Right now, can summon only 10 ice cubes at a time). Element; Ice. Power Personality; Tricker. Got the quirk from her mother. Level, 2.4- Mid Tier. Has green eyes and red hair. In a short story about her nickname; Mouny always gets angry at small things. As she gets angry, she becomes hot like the sun. And, the

temperature of the sun comes in positive, which is a plus sign. So, her cousins started to call her Plus. And so it became her nickname.

About Daniel Wendon:-

Daniel's nickname is Rain. Born on 20th February 2004, an 18-year-old student, His quirks; Main- Summon lightning strike and can control. (Right now, can control it and make it move a little bit). Element; Electric. Power Personality; Attacker. Got the quirk from his father. Branch- Summon a fire sword. (Right now, can defend himself from any attacks). Element; Fire. Power personality; Attacker. Got the quirk from his mother. Level, 2.6- Mid Tier. Has Indigo eyes and grey hair and a hairstyle with the electric sign. A short story about his nickname; Daniel once summoned the lightning strike, at that time rain also started, he enjoyed it and then, monsoon became his favorite season and his cousins started to call him Rain. And so it became his nickname.

CHAPTER III

The S.P (Superpower) High School

The next day, Anita went to her high school, she was sitting on her bench, until... A girl came near her, Anita saw her and it was Anupma! "Hi~," Anupma said, "Daisy?" Anita asked, "Yes!" Anupma replied, "So you are from this class? Didn't know it..." Anita said, "Yes. I am from this class. You are a new student here?" Anupma asked, "Yes! Yesterday was my first day here. But, I didn't see you yesterday, why so?" Anita asked, "Oh, yesterday I was unwell so I didn't come," Anupma said, "Oh..." Anita replied. "What about Rain plus? Do they also study here?" Anita asked, "Yes, they are in the other section," Anupma said, "Can we meet them now?" Anita asked, "Sure!" Anupma said, and they went to Rain plus's class. Anita entered the class, "He...llo?" She said, she saw Daniel was angry, "Bro! Chill out!" Mouny was saying. "Hello, Rain plus!" Anita said, "Hello crete," Mouny said, and Rain blushed, "Rain, why were you angry?" Anita asked, "I don't know what you are talking about," Daniel said, Mouny had an annoyed face, "Ok bye, I have to go!" Daniel said and went away. "What happened to Rain?" Anupma asked, "Rain is angry," Mouny said, "But why?" Anita asked, "Rain's friend was beaten by someone!" Mouny said, "Really?!" Anita and Anupma were surprised, "Yeah..." Mouny replied, "That's why he was angry," Mouny said, "Is Rain's friend okay now?" Anita asked, "Hell No!" Daniel said, and he came back. "I am going to kill that person who bet my buddy!" Daniel said angrily. "Chill out!" Anupma said, "Rain, take care of yourself also..." Anita said, she looked at Anupma and said, "Daisy let's go back to class," "Yeah!" Anupma replied, and they went outside. While they were going, Anita bumped into someone, "I am sorry, I didn't mean to bump you!" Anita apologized, "Are you blind?!" The boy who Anita bumped shouted. "There are so many stupid people in this high school" The boy murmured... Anupma witnessed this incident, and she was very angry at the boy, "Why was he so grumpy? You just bumped into him, and he acted like you did a shameful act!" Anupma said, "Yeah, I agree!" Anita replied, and they went to their class and sat on their bench. Later, they heard a lot of news, "Do you know Gloria? I heard she was beaten! Many are saying that she was beaten by the same guy who bet Keith!" A student said, "Keith? That is Rain's friend who was beaten by someone today! That guy is beating more children!" Anupma said, "But why is that boy doing this? Why is he beating all these children? For some revenge?" Anita asked, "Who knows!" Anupma replied. During the lunch break, Rain and plus came to Anupma and Anita's class. "Hello!" Rain and plus said, "Hello! By the way, have you both heard any news about a boy who is beating some children?" Anupma asked, "Beating children? Including Keith?" Daniel asked, "Yes..." Anupma said, Daniel became angry and tried to control his anger. "We haven't heard any news related to this" Mouny said, "Well, you should know about this now! No one doesn't know who he is, or how he looks-" Anupma said, "That is so weird!" Anita said in the middle. "How can no one know who is the culprit? The victim would have seen his face, right?" Anita continued, "That's the problem! The victims said they forgot his face... this is becoming suspicious!" Anupma said, "But why are we worrying about this? He didn't beat us!" Mouny said, "You are right, plus, but don't forget, one of the victims was Keith, Rain's friend, we should worry about him," Anita said, "I agree with you!" Anupma said. Suddenly, two children came toward them, "Guys! Have you heard about Louis?" They asked, "Louis? The strongest student in our class with level 3.3?" Anupma asked, "Yes! He was also bet by the same guy who bet Keith and Gloria!" They said, "What? Are you serious!?" Mouny asked, "Yes I am! Louis is hospitalized for 1 week- no, a whole month!" They said, "WHAT?!" All were shocked, "This guy is getting out of hand! We need to stop him!" Anita said, "Yeah, I totally agree!" Anupma said, and the children looked outside, "Is that? Is that your cousin, Rain?" they asked? "My cousin?" Anupma was confused, she looked outside and saw Daniel was injured, she was surprised, "Guys! Let's go outside..." Anupma said, they went outside, "Rain? What happened to you?" Mouny asked, "I fought with someone..." Daniel replied, "Fought with someone? With whom?" Mouny asked impatiently, "I... don't remember..." Daniel replied, "How can you don't remember the face with whom you fought just now?!" Mouny said angrily, Anita tried to calm her, "It's not my problem that I forgot the face!" Daniel said angrily, "Oh crap! Guys, now don't start arguing here, let's go to our class before this lunch break end, and then, everyone went to their class. "All victims... they all don't remember his face!" Anita murmured, Anupma heard it and said, "You still thinking about that? We will solve that later, now get ready for the next class!" "Okay..." Anita replied. The school ended, everyone packed their bags and went out of the class, Anita and her friends went outside, Anita again bumped into someone and it was the same person who she bumped in the morning, "You again?!" The boy said angrily, "I am sorry, it was a coincidence that we met again, I didn't mean to bump into you on purpose..." Anita apologized, "This apology will be accepted on only one condition! Let's duel each other!" The boy said, "What?!" Anita was confused, she got hit by something and she started to feel unconscious... A few minutes later, she woke up, "Are you okay, crete?" Her friends asked, "Where am I?" Anita asked, "You are in the big tree of our school," Anupma said, "What happened to me?" Anita asked, "We also don't know, you were laying down in the corridor of the ground floor, we tried to wake you up, but you weren't! So we brought you here and waited for you to wake" Mouny said, "Oh... but thanks for bringing me here and waiting for me!" Anita said, "And, blood was coming from your back, we checked and saw you had a wound! And then, I healed it. Were you in a fight? Or maybe fought the strange guy...?" Anupma asked, "A wound in my back... I don't remember a thing... but, maybe I bumped into someone, he told me to do a duel ad then... I forgot everything!" Anita said, all were shocked! "Crete! You didn't realize it, you bumped into that strange guy only!" Mouny said, "WHAT?!" Anita was shocked, "It's already 3 PM, your mother will be worried about you, so let's go home," Anupma said, they took a bus and went home. Anita and her friends went to their house, "Crete! What took you so long? What happened?" Anita's mother asked, "Mom! Daisy, plus and rain! All studies in my high school!" Anita said, "Oh, that's great, but what took you so long to come?" She again asked, "Mom! I also don't know! Umm... yeah! I bumped into someone on my way back home, he told me to duel and then he hit me and... I got unconscious" Anita said, "Hit you?? Who was it?" She asked angrily, "Mom, I don't know, I forgot his face, but! Something strange was happening in the high school! A strange kid was beating random children! And maybe, it included me and Rain... and more surprisingly! All the victims don't remember his face! This is so weird, right?"

Anita said, “Yes, it is very weird... Now go freshen up!” Her mother said, “Okay mom!” Anita replied.

CHAPTER IV

The strangest case (Strange guy beating random children)

Anita went to freshen up, washed her face, changed her clothes, sat on the sofa, grabbed the T.V remote, and started to watch the T.V. She switched the channel to the news channel, and saw, people were talking about S.P high school. “Mom! Look, the news is about my high school!” Anita said to her mother, “Really? Let me see also!” Her mother replied, she went to the living room and saw the T.V, “They are talking about that guy?” She asked, “Yeah...” Anita replied, “Now it’s getting too serious...” Anita’s mother said, “Yes mom... Wait, let me tell my friends also about this!” Anita said, and grabbed her cell phone, “Let me just call Daisy...” She murmured, dialed Anupma’s call, and called her, “Daisy!! You have to see this!!” Anita said, “What? What happened??” Anupma was confused, “Start your T.V! And switch to the news channel” Anita instructed, Anupma did as Anita told her to. Then, she was shocked, “What!? They are talking about our high school! ‘Strange guy beating random children’ hmm... So even police are trying to find him?” Anupma asked, “Yeah I guess so!” Anita replied, “Rain! Plus! Look at T.V!” Anupma told to her cousins, “What happened Daisy? Why are you shouting?” Mouny asked, and they both came to the living room, “Wait... this case, it is now spread to the whole city? Everyone knows about this??” Daniel asked, “Yes!” Anupma said, Daniel and Mouny were shocked. “But who complained about this? I don’t think so, no one would dare to tell about this to the whole city! The children in our high school are just cowards, that's why!" Anupma said, "Hey, look! The principal!" Anita said, They looked at the T.V, "Wait, did the principal complain about this, can't believe..." Mouny said, Anita, heard it and asked, "Why you can't believe it?" "Crete, you don't know our principal, he is one of the hated people in the school! He doesn't care about his students! Doesn't treat them well and does everything which can make children angry and hate him!" Mouny explained, "Ok, now I understood..." Anita replied, "Anyways... we will talk later, Crete," Anupma said, "Okay" Anita replied and the call ended. "I wonder what next to happens tomorrow..." Anita thought, "I again bumped into someone and it was the same person whom I bumped in the morning," Anita thought and started to try to remember his face but she failed, "Was there someone present when I bumped into him?" Anita thought, "Yes! There was Daisy with me! I should her ask about this, and again tried to call her, "Hello Daisy?" Anita said, "Hello Crete, what happened?" Anupma asked, "Daisy, do you remember? Today morning, when we were going back to our classroom from Rain and plus's classroom, I bumped into someone, do you remember his face?" Anita asked, "Umm... I can remember everything except his face! I remember what he even told you, 'Are you blind?' He said this..." Anupma said, "I also remember these things, but not the face..." Anita replied, "Crete, I think this is a type of quirk!" Anupma said, "What do you mean by it?" Anita was confused, "Only the victims are forgetting his face but normal people don't because they didn't fight with him. Maybe, this forgetting the face is a tricker quirk?" Anupma asked, "Yeah! It can be... And thanks for this idea, I will try to know about this!" Anita said, "Okay bye!" Anupma said and the call ended.

Anita rushed to her mother and asked about this, "Crete, maybe your friend saying is true, but I am not an expert in quirks, but I will try my best to know about this quirk" Her mother said with a gentle smile, Anita was happy. At night, Anita went to sleep, but her mother wasn't, she promised her, she will find out about the quirk. Anita's mother's dream job was to become a teacher, she tried everything but as ill-luck, she could have, she wasn't qualified and she never became a teacher, but became a

simple housewife. Though she had many books about quirks, she searched and tried to find about that quirk.

About Anita's Mother:-

Her real name is Shradha Howard Hemishan. Born on 7th October 1978, a 43-year-old mother and a housewife. Her quirks; Main- Make an electric rope which gives damage. (Right now, can summon within the range of 100 meters and can summon 2 of them at the same time. And the level of damage is 10). Element; Electric. Power Personality; Attacker. Got the quirk from her father. Branch- she lost her branch quirk as she is above 40-years-old. Level; 5.1 (High Tier). Nickname: Wire. Has blue eyes and light olive hair.

It was already 10 PM, Anita went to sleep, but, as Shradha promised her daughter to find the quirk, she was still finding it. "Quirk? It was a tricker, right?" She thought. At last, she found it! But, heard some weird noises, Shradha got suspicious, she went in the direction from where the noises came. "Would it be Crete?" She thought. Shradha saw a man, she was shocked and grabbed him with her rope, "Who are you?" She asked, but the man didn't say a word. "I said! Who are you? Why have you come here?" She asked angrily, "Fine, he will not say. I will just give him some damage!" Shradha thought. Before she gives the damage, someone grabbed her neck, she was choking! Shradha tried to get away from it, but when she did, she ran away. "Wish I could invisible myself..." Shradha thought. "There are two people, I can say... one was the guy whom I grabbed and the other was the one who choked me! I have to capture them!" She thought and went to find them and when she found them, she grabbed them with her rope. "So..." Before Shradha could say a word, the rain started, "What is going on?! It's literally summer and the rain has started!" Shradha thought, and something fell into her eyes, she was not able to see and the 2 people ran away. A few moments later, Shradha was able to see, she saw the 1st man and captured him with her rope, the man struggled to get out, he saw some raindrops and touched them and it became something solid and threw it on Shradha, "That's strange... he touched the raindrops (which was liquid) and it became solid!" Shradha thought, still she was able to grab him snd gave damage, level:5, because of the damage, he became unconscious. "Now, I have to find the other guy..." Shradha thought. Shradha thought. She went inside to find the other guy, she saw the guy had the books about quirks, she was shocked and tried to catch him, she caught him and gave some damage, but something grabbed her hand and so, the guy escaped, "NO! He ran away!" Shradha thought. She saw the book's page was torn away, "No..." She said. "Wait... there is something written, not remembering someone's face...is a quirk! Daisy was right. This quirk is an... organism element? What is that? And it is a tricker! I never heard of this quirk" Shradha thought, then, she took her phone and called the cops, a few minutes later, the cops came and arrested the 1st guy, "Excuse me, Miss!" A cop called Shradha, "Yes Sir" She replied, "So you have called us?"

He asked, "Yes Sir, because the guy and his friends broke onto my house and even tried to kill me!" Shradha said, "I see... Thank you miss for reporting to us!" He said, "Sir! I also have some information about the quirk!" Shradha said, "Really? Can you tell us?" The cop asked, "Sure, I can tell!" She replied and told him about the quirk. He was shocked after hearing it, "Thank you, miss, for this information!" The cop said, and he went away... Shradha was feeling sleepy and so she went inside and slept. The next morning, Anita woke up, and got ready for school, "Mom! I have a question for you..." She said to her mother, "Ask, crete" Shradha said, "Yesterday, last night, did something happen? Because I saw cops coming to our house, what happened yesterday, mom?" "Crete... well, some robbers broke into our house, and I fought with them, and I won! Then, I

called the cops to arrest them, but unfortunately, one of them ran away..." Shradha said, "Really? You fought with them?!" Anita asked, "Yes, crete!" Shradha replied, Anita was surprised. "Crete, it's time to go to school! Bye..." Shradha said, "Ok mom! Bye!" Anita said and she went to her high school.

CHAPTER V

I became a friend of snakes

Anita went to her class and met with her friends. It was 2nd period and the teacher hasn't come yet. "Do you think Mr. Isaac our maths teacher would come today?" Anupma asked, "I don't think so, I mean the second period is going to end also!" Anita replied. Suddenly, a teacher came to their class, "Children, this is a sad thing... but, your maths teacher would not be able to school for a month..." The teacher said all children were happy, "Yay! No maths class for a month!!" A student shouted, "But don't be so happy, the reason why he wouldn't be able to come to school is that the student bet Isaac also!" The teacher said and went away, all children were in shock, "T-that guy even bet Mr.Isaac?!" The children were saying, Anita was not happy hearing it, "More than 5 people! This guy is a psycho!" She said and became angry, "Crete! Calm down!!" Anupma said and tried to calm her, "Daisy! How am I supposed to be calm?! He bet me, Rain, our schoolmates, and now! Our maths teacher! And you are telling me to be angry?! Hell Nah!" Anita said angrily, Anupma was worried about Anita. Anita went near her classmates and asked them something, "Hello, just want to ask a question, what is Mr.Isaac's level?" She asked, "He is 3.5, an elite tier, a loser like you!" The children said and started laughing, Anita tried to calm herself and she went away. Anupma walked toward Anita and asked, "Crete, what are you doing?" "Trying to find that guy..." She replied, "You think you will find him that easily?" Anupma said, "I know... I am trying my best..." Anita said. Time passed too fast... it was lunch break, Anita went to meet her friends, suddenly she saw a boy who was looking sad, Anita went toward him and asked him, "Hey! Why are you looking so sad? Do you have any friends?" "Uhh... Well, I don't have any friends and that's why I am sad..." The boy said, "Oh... it's so sad, I can be your friend! I am Anita Hemishan, nice to meet you!" Anita said, "I am Harry Nash, nice to meet you, Anita!" Harry said, "Come, Harry, I will meet you with my other friends, then you can get more friends!" Anita said joyfully, seeing her, Harry smiled, "So Harry, from which class are you from?" Anita asked, "I am... from class C," Harry said, "Oh... how unlucky, I am from class A and my 2 friends are from class B, it would be nice if you would have been in class A or B, right?" Anita asked, "Yeah..." He agreed, "Harry, don't be shy! You should have the confidence to do something, once you lose your confidence, you lose everything!" Anita told Harry, and he nodded. "Look! My friends are there..." Anita pointed toward her friends. "Guys! This is my new friend, Harry Nash" Anita introduced them to him... They treated Harry nicely and he was happy, after eating their food, they started to talk to Harry, "Harry! Why you don't tell about yourself, from where have you come..." Mouny said, "I am from a very small village called, Sneer Forest. There, I had 2 friends, they were my best friends! But my father had to transfer here and our friendship broke..." Harry said, "That's very sad!" All said, "Oh no! The lunch break is going to be over, let's go to our class before the bell ring!" Daniel said and they went to their class. After school, all 5 friends were talking with each other happily, Harry remembered something when he was at Sneer Forest, he used to be happy with his old friends like he does now... Harry again felt happiness. "See you tomorrow, Harry, bye!" They said and all went to their home. Meanwhile, when Harry was going to his home, someone stopped him, "Harry, this is your last chance!" The guy said and went away... Anita told her mother everything that happened in the school, "Mom! Today I made a friend! His name is Harry Nash, he looked very sad and so I became friends with

him! My friends also became his friend, whenever we talk with each other, Harry look very happy!" She said, "That's good to hear!" Her mother replied. Harry reached his home looking sad, a few minutes later, he started to cry... "WHY! Why am I again involved in this type of thing? 6 years ago, I was falsely accused of murder, and now! That guy wants me to kill them!" Harry thought...

6 years ago, at Sneer Forest, there were three friends, Harry, and his two best friends, once they were playing in the park. Suddenly, they smelled something disgusting, so they went to that way where the smell was coming. And it was a dead body of a person! , the three children were in shock, "We should call the cops!" Harry said, "Yes!" His friends replied, Harry called the cops, and when they arrived... "So children, where is the corpse?" The cop asked, "It is here Sir. Also, we saw with our eyes that our friend whom we thought was innocent, killed this guy! We are the witness!!" They said it was a bolt from the blues, "I-I am speechless! This is not true sir! I don't even know this guy! Why would I kill him? Guys, what the heck? Why would you accuse me of a fake murder?!" Harry said, he already knew it, his 'best friends' betrayed him, "I became a friend of snakes?" Harry thought, Sneer Forest was a very small village and cops usually don't follow the laws, they didn't check any evidence and handcuffed Harry. According to the police, he will be imprisoned for a year... But you might think, why did his friends betray him? His friends think they were better than Harry, that's why they started to act

rude and always negative toward him, making him think, his friends are his good friends, but always leave him alone, and always asked help from Harry but never helped him back, and started to hate him, and didn't want him in their life anymore, so instead of breaking the friendship, they falsely accused him. That day, Harry's heart was broken, he cried as much as he could. The next day, his parents came to meet him at the police station and as expected, they were disappointed in him. "Son, what happened to you? How can this happen?" They asked many questions... "Everyone has only mouths to say, but not a pair of ears to hear," Harry thought, he tried to explain to his parents about it. A few minutes later, they understood that he is falsely accused. Harry's parents will not get any lawyer in the village so they wouldn't be able to bail out their son. He had to stay at the police station for a year, staying away from his family. A year later, the day came, Harry will no more stay in the prison, he went home and met his parents. "Son, Sneer Forest is not what it used to be, for us now..." Harry's father said, "What do you mean, dad?" Harry asked, "You were right, Everyone has only mouths to say, but not a pair of ears to hear. There is a big gossip about you. You are the youngest criminal here... which is not true! I know, but who is going to believe us? All are 'hating' us, people said so many bad things to us! We can't live here, we are going to Super Town tomorrow, so help your mother in preparing!" His father explained, "Okay dad..." Harry replied. The next day, they left Sneer Forest. But, at Super Town, no one cared about Harry and became friends with him. Harry used to be lonely and see other children playing with their friends... "They are very lucky!" He says and smiles... and spends all his days alone.

"I wonder what will he do with me if I didn't kill them... I don't care also. Why would I kill innocent people?" Harry told himself. The next day, his mother woke him up, "Harry! Why are we getting threats from... this strange guy?" She asked, Harry was in shock, "Wait, mom didn't I tell you about that guy? He is doing this!" Harry said, "But why?" Her mother asked, "To make me work for him! I can't explain the whole thing, I will tell you after school!" Harry said and went to get ready... After reaching the school, the guy came to meet Harry, "Harry! You can't do a thing! If now, you didn't kill them, then you will die!" He said and went away..."Everyone thinks I am their worker! I will not kill them, they are my new friends and I will... no! I will never!" Harry thought. Anita and her friends came to meet Harry and they started to talk, a few minutes later, "Guys, I have to go to the washroom, so wait a minute!" Harry said and went to the washroom, his friends were waiting for him, it was already half an hour and he didn't come back yet, "I think we can meet him at the break... he is not coming back" Anita said, all agreed and they went to their class.

CHAPTER VI

Fame and popularity: Greg

A boy went to the washroom and started shouting, "THERE IS A BODY!! A DEAD BODY!!" Everyone heard it, everyone went there, and it was Harry, Daniel was in shock, "Harry? Is he dead?" He asked, the boy nodded. Daniel was completely blank... He couldn't believe it, "H-Harry died? But I met him yesterday, only!" He thought, He left the washroom with a sad face, and went to his class. "Rain! Who's corpse was it?" Mouny asked, "Harry..." Daniel replied, "Harry? No way! Is this true?" Mouny asked, "IT IS!!" Daniel said, Mouny became sad... During the lunch break, Daniel and Mouny told everything to Anita and Anupma, they had the same reaction as everyone. Anita was very sad, "Harry, he became our new friend and! Today he died! We didn't even get time to know about him, not even his quirks!" Anita said, all were sad because of Harry's death, "May Harry Nash rest in peace..." All said. Suddenly, Harry's mother came to high school, she asked the children about Harry, Anita saw her and said, "Aunt! I know him! I became friends with him yesterday!" "You are Anita, right? My son told me about you... Well, do you know where is my son?" She asked, "Aunt, unfortunately, your son, Harry died today... at the washroom," Anita said, "What!!?? HOW? WHEN?!" Harry's mother panicked, "Aunt! Be calm, we had the same reaction as you..." Anupma said, Harry's mother started to cry, "He was going to say me something... Why? Is my son that unlucky?!" She said all tried to calm her, "Wait. He was going to say you something, what was it?" Mouny asked, "It was about the strange guy... He was making my son work for him!" Harry's mother said, "Strange guy? What is he up to? Before, he used to beat children, and now making them work, what is going on?!" Anupma said. All were very confused, "Children, I need some time to deal with this truth. Please excuse me..." Harry's mother said and went away with tears in her eyes. "That strange guy! He is ruining everyone's life! I wish, I could meet him and beat him to death!!" Anita said angrily, "Crete! Don't forget it, he also defeated an elite tier, you are just a mid-tier, think what he can do with you!" Anupma explained, and all went to their class. Meanwhile, Anita went to the washroom, and while going back to the class, she saw a snake, at first she was surprised and then smiled and said, "Look, a small friend trying to attack me!" She said to herself and summoned a small wall at the top of the snake, and the snake died instantly, Anita pretended as if nothing happened and started to go to her class. Suddenly, someone interprets her walk, "Hello..." The person said, "Who are you? Can you move, I need to go back to my class..." Anita said and wasn't interested in the guy, "You are Anita, right? Nice to meet you, Anita Hemishan" The person said, She was in shock, "How do you know my name?" She asked, "My name is Gregory Oak, you don't know but I know you. We are from the same town! Claytown!" Gregory said, "Ohh! I didn't know it. Hello, nice to meet you, Gregory, I also think, I heard this name" Anita said, "Yes! I also heard your name many times... the defender, the children used to call you that" Gregory said, "Yeah" Anita replied. Suddenly, Gregory attacked Anita with his quirk, "Yo! Chill!" Anita said she didn't want to fight with him so she invis herself and went away. "What happened to Gregory suddenly? He was acting friendly and then attacked me...." Anita thought.

About Gregory Oak:-

Also known as Greg. Born on 7th August 2004, a 17-year-old student, His quirks; Main- summon any type of snake and control them (right now, can summon only 1 snake at a time and control it). Element; Earth. Power Personality; Attacker. Got the quirk from his mother. Branch- Can summon papers of any length. (Right now, summon paper with a length of 5 meters.). Element; Paper. Power personality; Tricker. Got the quirk from his father. Level, 2.6- Mid Tier. Has dark green eyes and indigo hair.

Anita told Anupma about Gregory, "Gregory... I heard this name" Anupma said, "Let us ask Rain and pus, they might know it" She continued, and Anita agreed with her and they went to their class. "Do you both know who is Gregory Oak?" Anita asked them, "Oh... that popular kid, I know him," Daniel said with an uninteresting face, "Popular kid? But, what is up with this uninteresting face?" Anita asked, "Oh well... you see, as Greg being the 'popular kid' many people like him, so he is just jealous," Mouny said, Anita and Anupma started after hearing it. "Well, it's obvious also!" Anupma said, "Okay... so, Gregory Oak is the popular kid here?" Anita asked, "Yeah!" Daniel replied, "Okay! Thanks for this information!" Anita said and went away with Anupma. Anita was thinking about Gregory, "We are from the same town! Claytown!" She thought, "Daisy! I want to meet him..." Anita said, "What? Do you mean Greg? You can meet him later..." Anupma replied, "Just tell me what is his class," Anita said, "He is in class C," Anupma said, "C... Like Harry" Anita said, "Yeah..." Anupma replied. Anita wanted to know more about Gregory, she tried to ask about him to her classmates, "Hey, can I ask you something?" She asked, "Sure" They replied, "Do you know anything about Gregory Oak? I heard he is a popular kid" Anita said, her classmates started laughing, "First of all, how did you know about him? And, why do you want to know about him?" They asked, "Today, at the lunch break, he came to me and talked with me, that's how I know him. I want to know about him because he said, we are from the same town" Anita said. Hearing this, all were in shock and were speechless, "Hey! Listen up, we don't believe you, so, stop making these stories! He will never go to you and ask to talk to you!" They said. Anupma was watching it, she knew an argument was gonna start so she went near them. "I don't care if you believe me or not. I just wanted my answer, so if you please answer it, then this stupid argument which you want to start will end before it starts!" Anita said calmly, Anupma was seeing all these. They rolled their eyes and said, "Yeah, we know him" They said. "Do you know why is he so popular?" Anita asked, "Didn't you see him? Of course! Because of his handsome face! That's why everyone likes him. He is not ugly as you, that's why you are not popular, as him! Many 'boys' are also jealous of him, including your new friend, Rain! Can you tell him, he is ugly, don't be jealous of Greg!" They said, "Okay... popular just because of his face, handsome? Hmm... What did you also say? I am ugly, I will never become popular like Greg? Just wait, I will solve this mystery and maybe I will, you never know! And... Rain, he is ugly? Then what are you? People like you are the ones, who can't see the real beauty! If he is really ugly, I don't care what people think about him! He is my friend, not a thing! You people just judge people by the outside, he looks ugly, weird, so he is not a good guy! Can't even see the beauty inside..." Anita said, all were speechless. Anupma was surprised, "Crete! Did you just defend Rain, why?" Anupma asked, "Rain is a nice guy. He is also my friend, I don't want anyone to talk about my friends! Rain is a shy guy, people can make fun of him easily. You see, when I was in Claytown, I was just like him! Shy and easily getting bullied, there was no one to defend me, except my mom. I don't want to happen the same things to Rain. And it will also show how good a friend I am!" Anita said with a smile. Anupma was happy to hear this, "Thank you, Crete! You are a lot better friend than I thought! You defended my cousin which I never did! Thank you so much!" Anupma

said, Anita, laughed and said, "It's nothing, if you are a good friend then it would be probably one of your habits!" "Yeah, I agree!" Anupma said. The school ended, Anita and her friends went to their home, and on the way, they met Gregory, "Greg!" Anita said to him, "Anita?" He asked, "I wanted to meet you!" Anita said, and they started to talk, Anita's friends saw them, "Let's just leave them here and let's go," Mouny said, "Yeah! She also said to me, that we can go without her" Anupma added, but Daniel wasn't looking happy seeing them...

CHAPTER VII

Jealousy! It's Jealousy!!

Daniel was staring at them, Mouny and Anupma saw him and asked, "Bro! Why are you staring at them like this? It's like you are gonna kill them!" "I Will!!" He replied, "What!?" They asked, "Umm..." Daniel said, "Rain, you are looking jealous! Is it because of Greg?" Anupma asked, "Yeah! Look! Anita is looking very happy talking with him..." Daniel said sadly, "So? Then why is it hurting you? I am very happy seeing them" Anupma said, "Daisy, you stupid! Did you forget already?" Mouny said to Anupma, "Ohh! I understood!" She replied, "Let's just go away from here..." Daniel said with an uninteresting tone, "Umm... Okay!" Mouny and Anupma replied. Meanwhile, Gregory saw Daniel is feeling jealous, he asked, "That is your friend? Why did you befriend an ugly guy?" And started laughing, "Did you just make a joke? I didn't hear it" Anita replied, Gregory was speechless, "I know people like you! Stop making fun of Daniel. I can't take all these insults of him!" Anita said with a serious tone, "Okay! Just chill!" Gregory said. Daniel was not able to see them, he went away without his cousins, he was sad... Anita saw him, she wasn't looking happy seeing him go away. "We will meet tomorrow, bye!" Anita said to Gregory and went to Mouny and Anupma, and asked, "What happened to Rain? Why did he go away without you?" "Umm..." They were silent, "Why are you silent? Tell me something!" Anita asked, "He was not happy seeing you talking with Gregory... b-because, he is jealous of him! He hates him!" Mouny said, "Hmm..." Anita thought, "Or, just ask him by yourself!" Anupma said with a big smile, "Sure! I will ask him this evening!" Anita said, "Yes! You should!!" Anupma said, "Why are you so happy?" Mouny whispered to Anupma, "If Crete asks Rain about this, then he will not get any chance, but to tell her! He has to confess it!" Anupma asked, "Ohh... I see!" Mouny replied, "What are you guys talking about?" Anita asked, "Nothing, let's go home!" They said and went to their home. It was evening, all went to the park and met each other. "Rain, what happened to you today? Why did you go home alone?" Anita asked, "Umm..." Daniel said, "Say it! Say it!" His cousins said, "I was feeling jealous! You looked so much happy while talking with Greg, and with me, you don't! And also..." Rain said, "NO! It's not true! I feel happier talking with you, forget about Greg! He was talking trash about you, don't feel jealous of him!" Anita said, "Oh..." Daniel said and blushed, "Anyways, let's play!" Anita said, Mouny and Anupma were disappointed, "No! This was such a good chance!" Anupma said, "Yeah..." Mouny agreed. And they started to play. The next day, they went to the high school. Daniel met Gregory, "You are Rain, right?" Gregory asked him, "Yes..." Daniel replied, "You were also a victim of the strange guy?" He asked, "Yeah..." Daniel replied, "Okay! Have a nice day..." Gregory said and went away, later he met with Anita, Daniel was watching them, and noticed something suspicious, he saw Gregory was trying to come closer to Anita, Daniel didn't like it, he went towards him and asked, "Greg, can you talk with Anita in a distance, I think you are too close to her" Daniel said, "Yeah, I also feel like that" Anita agreed with him, "Bro! What is your problem? Why do you always come in between me and Crete? Is it because you are jealous of me?" Gregory asked, "Stop talking trash!" Daniel said angrily, "I dare you! Just try to attack me!" Gregory said, "Greg! Don't start an unnecessary fight!" Anita tried to stop, "People like you can only shut their mouths by some slaps! And I can give you!" Daniel

said. Anita already knew this argument wouldn't stop so she kept silent and was listening to it. "Bro! Just admit it! You are jealous of me!" Gregory said, "Okay I will! But, stop talking trash about it!" Daniel said, "Fine! Then, let's have a duel! The one who loses will shut his mouth forever!" Gregory said, "Rain! There's no chance you are gonna win that duel! Stop it..." Anita said to Daniel, "Crete! Don't forget, he was making you uncomfortable, you will keep silent? If you don't take any actions, then I will!" Daniel said angrily, Anita was silent, she never saw Daniel that angry, "Oh? So you already accepted your death?" Gregory said, "Man, just shut up!" Daniel said, "You think I will?" Gregory said. The duel began! Everyone went to see the duel. Daniel vs Gregory, who would win it?

Daniel had the first move, he tried to attack Gregory with a combat attack, so he summoned his fire sword and tried to strike him. Gregory wasn't able to defend himself, and got some damage... The next move was Gregory's, he summoned his paper, tried to capture him by it, but failed! He looked back and saw Daniel with his fire sword and! Gave another attack with it. Gregory summoned a snake and it bites Daniel! And it was a poisonous snake! Before something could happen to him, he strikes a lightning strike on Gregory, he got a lot of damage, Gregory summoned his paper and grabbed Daniel, and threw him to the ground, no one was able to understand who will win the duel. Daniel was not moving, and Anita became worried, "So... look likes-" Gregory was going to finish his line and before he could, Daniel strikes another lightning strike on him, all were in shock. Gregory fell to the ground... and so Daniel... "Who's the winner?" Everyone asked, "Everyone saw it, Gregory was the one who fell to the ground first and then Rain. It is clear! Rain won the duel!!" Anita said happily, and everyone agreed with her. Anita ran towards Daniel, she saw he was unconscious, and called Mouny and Anupma for help, "Daisy, heal him!" Anita said, Anupma started to heal him, Mouny brought water for him, a few seconds later, Daniel woke up, they were happy. "Who won the duel?" Daniel asked, "YOU!!" Anita said happily and hugged him. Daniel blushed, and Mouny and Anupma smiled seeing them. "Let's go to the class!" Daniel said and others agreed. They went towards their class. Meanwhile, Anita's classmates heard about the duel. "Have you heard about the duel? Daniel vs Gregory?" One of them asked, "Yeah! I also heard that ugly Daniel won!" Another one said, "But do you know the reason for the duel?" The first one asked, "No? What was it?" Another one asked, "Remember Anita? Greg was making her uncomfortable, so Daniel became angry and said to not make her again, but Greg didn't listen to him and so the duel started... Daniel is a lot different than we thought!" The first one said, "Yeah... we thought he is a bag and weird guy, but... he fought for Anita! I still can't believe, we used to think about him!" Another one said, "Anita is very lucky! No one would ever do that for me!" "Yeah... I agree" They said. "Umm... there is still time, let's apologize Anita for making fun of Daniel!" "Okay!" They decided to apologize and went to Anita... "Hey! Anita! We are very sorry for what we did yesterday. We are apologizing for making fun of your friend, Daniel" They said, "What is up with these apologies?" Anita asked, "People blindfolded us! We were not able to see the truth! We thought, Rain is a weird guy, but, he is a good guy"

They said, “Are you jealous or something?” Anita asked, “NO! Why would we be? We are feeling happy for you, for having such a good friend” They replied, “Okay! I forgave you for your yesterday’s act! Please don’t do it again or with someone else” Anita said, “Okay, we will never” They said and smiled. They went away... “Wow, Crete! I am not able to believe it! The people who used to bully you from day 1, apologized for that! I have never seen this!” Anupma said, “Well, you have seen it today!” Anita replied. “They said I am lucky...” Anita said, “Really? That’s true also! Friends like Rain are difficult to find!” Anupma said, “Yeah, I know...” Anita replied. Suddenly, Anita started laughing, Anupma asked, “What happened? Why are you laughing?” “Remember how Rain used to be jealous of Greg?” Anita asked, “Yeah!” Anupma replied, “His way of speaking when we talk about Greg, would be always jealous tone!” Anita said, “Yeah... Crete, do you think Rain is interesting??” Anupma got the chance and asked, “Yeah, of course, anyone can like him!” Anita answered, “So... do you?” Anupma asked, “Umm...” Anita was speechless and blushed, “I don’t think, I would have an answer for this. But, maybe wait some years or months to know the answer!” Anita said, “Okay!” Anupma replied.

CHAPTER VIII

Helping the police

Anita and Anupma went to their class, on their way, Daniel interrupted and asked Anita, "Crete! Do you want to solve the mystery of the strange guy?" "Yeah..." She replied, "Well, I heard the police are now taking the action! So, you could help them" Daniel said, "Oh... Sure, I would like to" Anita said, "After school, you can meet them, I will call you!" Daniel said, Anita agreed with him, and they all went to their class. Gregory was staring at them, he wasn't happy after losing the fight with Daniel, he wanted revenge from them. He walked away... After school, they all went to their home. As usual, Anita told her mother about today, "Mom! And, then, Rain defeated him! The bullied apologized to me, today was such a good day" Anita said, "I knew it! Rain is such a good guy..." Her mother said, "Yeah, mom" Anita replied. A couple of hours later, Daniel came to Anita's house. "Hello Rain, what brings you here?" Anita's mother asked him, "Look, she forgot to mention it! Crete is helping the police in finding the strange guy from our high school. I told her, that I will call her so here I am!" Daniel said, "Ohh! My daughter is doing such a good thing" She said, "Yeah! Now, can you call her?" Daniel asked, "Sure, just wait a minute" She replied and went to call Anita. A few minutes later, she came and they went to the police station. "Evening. So, you want to help us?" The police asked, "Yes!" Anita replied, "What was your name again?" The police asked, "Anita Hemishan" Anita said, "Hemishan? I have heard this name... What was that name? Sharadha H. Hemishan-" The police said to himself,

"That's my mother's name!" Anita said, "Oh. Your mother also came to the police station, you know?" The police asked, "Yes, some 'robbers' people broke into our house..." Anita said, "Robbers? But your mother didn't mention anything about 'robbers" The police said, Anita started thinking, "What? Didn't mention robbers? Does this mean the robbers didn't come to our house? Mom will never do this, if they would have came, mom would have told the police, but mom didn't... I need to know what really happened that night!" She thought. "Anita, can you tell how many people he bet?" The police asked. "7 people" Anita replied. "Child, can you do a favor for us? You have to find the biodata of these victims, can you?" The police asked, "Sure! I can" Anita replied. "Well, we don't need any help other than these... if we need, then Rain will call you" The police said, "You know rain?" Anita asked, "Yes, he is my nephew. I am plus's father, you are her friend, I know it, nice to meet you" The police said and smiled. "Nice to meet you, Mr. Reshan," Anita said, "You can go now," The police said, and Anita went away. She went home. "What did the police ask?" Her mother asked, "How many people did the strange guy bet?" Anita replied, "That's all?" Her mother asked, "Yeah... and also told to find the biodatas of these victims" Anita said. "Mom, that day when the robbers came. That day, did robbers come?" Anita asked, "I think, it's time to tell you the truth. That day, no robbers broke into our house, it was 2 normal people. They tried to kill me. Also, your mother is a victim of the strange guy. One of them was him because I also forgot his face" Anita's mother said. "WHAT!! YOU ARE ALSO A VICTIM!!??" Anita was shocked, "Yes! Now calm down!" Her mother said and tried to calm her down. Anita told her friends, that her mother is also a victim, and they were also shocked as Anita was. She also told them about the work given by the police, "Good luck!" They said. The next day, Anita went to the high school and went to the staff room. "Gloria, Keith, Louis, Rain, me, Mr. Issac, and Harry... I need biodatas of these people, and I think, it would be here, in the staff room" Anita thought and asked the teachers about that, "I need biodata of classes A, B, C, and D. The police want that" Anita told them, "Anita, you started working with them? Good to hear, here they are" The teacher said, "Thank you so much. Also, I need the biodata of Mr. Issac" Anita said, "Wait a minute, here it is" The teacher said, Anita thanked her and went to her class, keeping all the biodatas in her bag, and went outside to meet her friends. She talked with them and went back to the class. After school, Anita went to the police station and gave the biodatas. "Thank you, Anita," The police said, "It's my pleasure" Anita replied and smiled. "Hmm... there is something common. All the victims are below LVL 3.0 except Mr. Issac who has LVL 3.5" The police said, "Does this mean the strange guy's LVL is above 3.2?" Anita asked, "Probably..." He replied. "Now, our task is to find the students whose levels are above 3.0, can you find them?" The police asked, "I will try..." Anita replied, "Thanks, you may now leave," The police said and Anita went away. She went to her house and told everything to her mother and friends. Anita was chatting with her friends in the group chat. "GUYS!! You need to help me with this task!" Anita messaged, "What is the task?" They asked, "I have to find the students whose levels are above 3.0" Anita messaged, "It is not an easy task! Because fewer children are above 3.0" Mouny messaged, Anupma agreed with her. "I will help you" Daniel messaged, "You can find in classes A and B, and I, will find it in the classes C and D" Daniel messaged, "Okay!" Anita replied. The next day, Anita and Daniel went to the staff room to find all children's biodatas. After many hours, of trying to find it, "There is a total of 15 students with a level above 3.0!" Anita said with a tired tone, "Let's take these biodatas..." Daniel said with a tired tone and they took the biodatas and went to their classes. Gregory saw Anita and Daniel in the corridor, he wasn't happy seeing them. "One day, I am gonna take revenge for my insult..." Gregory said to himself. Anupma and Mouny went to meet Anita and Daniel... "You guys bunked 2 periods! Wow!!" Anupma and Mouny said, "Wait, really we did?" They asked, "Yeah," Anupma and Mouny said. Anita and Daniel were in surprise. And they started talking... Meanwhile, Gregory went to the bathroom, and while returning, he met someone who covered his whole face, and that guy wore a mask and a hat and took him somewhere. Gregory remembered, how he met Anita, outside the bathroom, and they talked... A few seconds later, he noticed he was somewhere else. "Where am I?" Gregory asked, "You are Greg, the popular kid, right?" The guy asked, "WHO ARE YOU!!??" Gregory asked, "The strange guy," The guy said, Gregory was in shock, "I don't believe you!" Gregory said, "Man, just shut up. Listen up! You hate Anita, and so I do! I even know about your secrets... Should I tell the whole high school, your secret? In the Claytown... the child you used to be. You were a lot different from how you are! A child used to be bullied, a weak, ugly child. Imagine everyone knowing this, and what things would they think about you? So, do you want to save your respect from the students or-" The strange guy said, "Okay, don't tell anyone about this secret, please! What do you want?" Gregory asked, "I want you to defeat Anita, so team up with me," The strange guy said, "But I don't believe you, you are not that strange guy. You even covered your face! At least tell your name!" Gregory said, "I will not show you my face, nor I will tell you my name, tell something else to prove I am the strange guy," The strange guy said. Gregory thought and said, "If you again bet Daniel, then I will believe you are the strange guy!" He said, "Okay, wait till tomorrow morning..." The strange guy said and let Gregory go away. "I wonder if he is the real strange guy?" Gregory thought and went to his class. The school ends, and Anita went to the police station and said, "And here are the biodatas of the children" The police saw the biodatas. "Hmm... this child, Evan Hendam. He is having the same quirks as the person who tried to kill your mother!" The police said, "Does this mean Evan is the strange guy?" Anita asked, "We are not sure... he is just a suspect," The police said, "Oh..." Anita replied. "We have to talk with him!" The police said, "Thank you so much for your help, Anita!" The police said, "Happy to help!" Anita said and went to her home.

CHAPTER IX

Gregory, the new villain

The next day, Gregory went to the high school, "That guy told, 'wait till the morning, I don't believe him! If someone takes you somewhere and says, he is the most dangerous person in the high school, the strange guy! Who would believe him?" Gregory said to himself, on his way to his class, he saw Anita crying in the corridor. "What happened to her? Why is she crying? I guess I have to ask her to know the answer..." Gregory thought and went towards her, "Hey, Crete!" Gregory said to her, she sobbed and said, "Oh... Greg" "What happened to you? Why are you crying?" Gregory asked, "Do you not know? That strange guy! I want to kill him!! What's his problem? Why did he again bet Rain?? Because of him, Rain is now hospitalized!" Anita said, Gregory was shocked, "So... he really bet him!" Gregory thought, "Ohh... how sad," Gregory said, acting like he is sad for Daniel. "Rain is hospitalized for a day, but... Louis! Louis is hospitalized for 1 week- no, a whole month! And I don't think he has still come back yet. What is his problem?" Anita said angrily, "Uhh... I don't know. Crete, take care of yourself, wipe your tears off. I have to go, bye!" Gregory said, "Yeah, sure I will take care of myself. Bye..." Anita said and wiped her tears and Gregory went to his class, kept his bag, and went to the same place where the strange guy took him. He was finding him and finally, they again met. "Do you believe now I am the real strange guy?" The strange guy asked, "Yeah, I do now" Gregory replied. "Strange guy... I have a question for you, how did you know about my past? How do you know, I am from Claytown?" Gregory asked, "There's something called friends, that you don't have. But I can be" The strange guy replied. "Friends? What are you talking about? I didn't have any" Gregory replied. "Yes. But you do have classmates, right? I asked them" The strange guy said. "You went to Claytown? Wow!" Gregory said, the strange guy nodded.

Gregory is now a popular student, everyone likes him. But before, he was not like that. Gregory is from Claytown, and just like Anita, he also got bullied because of his face and personality. He was not happy hearing all these things about him. "Greg is a weird guy" "Look at him, doesn't even talk with anyone" "His face is so ugly," Everyone says about him. Gregory always thinks about these things and wasn't able to forget those words. Thinking about all those things, he wasn't able to sleep well, and well, he got dark circles and children bullied for that also. And, one day, he couldn't take this anymore and cry till the night, he was getting sick. Gregory told his parents to go to another city because he can't take this bullying and so they went to Super Town. The children were nice to him, he was getting enough sleep and the dark circles were also gone, he was very happy. But, he noticed everyone likes him because of his face. Gregory was happy seeing all these but... also sad because no one became his real friend. The girls liked him because of his face, but they never knew about him. "Will, they ever anyone see my personality?" Gregory always thinks. Soon, he forgot about it and was happy with his life. And just because of his handsome face, today Gregory is the popular kid in the high school.

"Okay, Strange guy, you can become my friend, but why do you want to?" Gregory asked, "Didn't I tell you yesterday? I want to take revenge on Anita, and so you do! Let's team up and defeat her" The strange guy said.

"Why do you want to defeat her?" Gregory asked, "Stop asking! Are you in my plan or not?" The strange guy asked, "Okay, I am in. What's the plan?" Gregory asked. "Today, you will attack her, during the lunch break. Today her rain hasn't come to the school, so no one will be there to defend her except herself, we will take advantage of that, you will attack! And, if her friends came to the fight, then I am here to back you up, what do you think?" The strange guy explained. "Okay? I guess..." Gregory replied. "Now, go to your class," The strange guy said, and Gregory went to his class. "Today is the day! Today is the revenge day!" Gregory thought and laughed evilly. It was the lunch break, he saw Anita... and he attacked her...

Gregory summoned a snake, the snake bite Anita, and he summoned the papers and choked her. Gave her some punches, and she started bleeding. Anita invis herself. Summoned a wall, made a rock from it, and threw it on Gregory, he looked back and saw Anita. He summoned the papers around her, grabbed her with the papers, took her up, and threw her on the ground. Anita wasn't able to do anything, she knew, she lost. Anita closed her eyes, she was unconscious. Gregory won the fight, he was very happy. "This fight was very easy!" Gregory said and went away, he thought to take a level test. "How can I defeat her so easily? She is LVL 2.7 and I am LVL 2.6, I should take a test" Gregory thought and took the test, he saw his level was 2.8! He was very shocked. And went to the strange guy's place. "Plan successful" Gregory said, The strange guy was happy, "Good job!" He said. "But what is up with my level? It is now 2.8, how?" Gregory asked but the strange guy ignored him. And, Gregory went away. Meanwhile, some children came to Anupma and Mouny and said, "Your friend!! She is in the corridor!!" They were surprised and ran towards the corridor, they saw Anita was laying down on the floor, "Omg, she got so many wounds!" Anupma said and started to heal her. "Was she in a fight?" Mouny asked the children, "Yeah! Gregory fought with her" The children said, "You were there?" Mouny asked, "Yes" They replied, "Then, why did you not stop the fight?" Mouny asked, "Have you ever seen people stopping a fight? We didn't want to get beaten" They replied. "Crete's all wounds are healed, but she is not going to wake up, someone bring water!" Anupma said. Mouny went to bring water, and came back with a glass of water, she sprinkled the water on Anita's face, and then, she woke up. "Where am I?" She asked. "You are in the school itself. Are you okay?" They replied. "Yeah, I am okay... my wounds? They are healed!" Anita said, "I healed it," Anupma said. "Why did Greg attack you?" They asked, "I... don't know," Anita said. "Now, let's go back to our class," They said and all went to their class. After school, Anita and her friends went to the hospital to meet with Daniel. "Rain! It's me, Crete" Anita said "Crete, how was the school?" Daniel asked, and they both started talking, "We can talk with Rain later..." Mouny said, and Anupma agreed with her. They went away. "It was not so nice! Greg attacked me out of nowhere, and he defeated me" Anita said sadly, "What? Did you got wounds?" Daniel said. "Of course! I was bleeding in my head. He also punched me. And threw me to the ground, because of that, my face got many wounds" Anita said. "Are you okay now?!" Daniel asked, "Don't worry! I am fine! Daisy healed me" Anita replied, "Rain, do you know why Greg attacked me? I don't know, why he did, do you?" Anita asked, "I know... A couple of days ago, I defeated him in the duel. He wanted to take revenge on me, but I didn't come today. The duel also started because of you, that's why he attacked you. He has taken his revenge" Daniel said. They both talked about school stuff and looked very happy talking with each other. A few minutes later, Anupma and Mouny came into the room and

talked with their cousin, and went to their home. Anita also went away... but, to the police station. "Good evening, Anita. I was waiting for you!" The cop said, "Good evening, what happened, sir? Did you get something?" Anita asked. "Yeah... I found many things, but first, answer me! Did you see Evan today?" The cop asked. "No, sir, I didn't" Anita replied. "This kid, Evan... is very strange!" The cop said. "Let me tell you what happened when we tried to find him," The cop said and narrated the adventure he and his team experienced.

CHAPTER X

The mysterious kid: Evan

"We wanted to meet the kid, so we went to the address which was given in his biodata as his 'home address'. We went there and found something unexpected! We knocked at the door, and... "This is the police," We said, and the door was opened by a man. "Are you the father of Evan Hendam?" We asked, "Who is that? I don't know any Evan!" The man said and we were in shock, "But, this is his house! He lives here, right?" We asked. "What? Look, mam and sir, no one lives here by the name of Evan! Only I live here!" The man said. "What's your name?" We asked, and we were very suspicious about him. "Bill George," The man said. "If Bill lives here, then where does Evan live?" We asked ourselves. "Mr. Bill, did you buy this house? Or rent or someone gave you?" We asked, "A couple gave me this house" Bill replied. "Couples... For how much?" We asked, "They gave me for free! I was a homeless beggar" Bill said, "Oh... do you remember the couple's name?" We asked, "Yes, their name was Diana Price Hendam and Matt Hendam" Bill replied. "Hendam, you say? I think they are Evan's parents" A cop said to us, and we agreed with her. We didn't had anything more to do, so we went away. Now, you have to help us! Can you find Evan? In your high school" The cop completed the story. "Okay, sir. I will try my best to find him" Anita said and went to her house. She thought a while... "How am I supposed to find him?" She asked herself, she seeks help from her friends. The next day, Anita went to her high school and told everyone about Evan, "If you see him anywhere! Just go straight to him and tell, 'Anita wants to meet you at the playground at 11:30 AM' Okay? Tell everyone! Your friends, your classmates. You guys should tell every student in this school, one of them would see Evan!" Anita told her classmates. The whole class started to talk about that topic, "Do you know? Anita wants to meet Evan, have you seen him?" They asked each other. Gregory was roaming around, Anita saw him, "Greg! Have you seen Evan?" She asked, "No, why do you want to meet him?" Gregory asked, "Because the police are suspecting him for the strange guy! Even his home address is fake! That guy is mysterious!!" Anita said, Gregory was shocked. "Evan is the strange guy? What!!??" Gregory thought. He went to the place where he meet the strange guy, but he was not there, "That guy is not here? Then where is he?" Gregory thought. Many children tried to find him by their quirks, but they failed. Evan was not there at the school. But, the police had pasted pictures of him outside and everywhere. Evan was running away from the high school, but the citizens saw him and took him to the police. The police called the victims. "So, this is the person? He is the strange guy? Can you all remember the face?" They asked. The victims said, "Yes...". "So, you are the strange guy?" The police asked, "Yeah! It's better to be in the jail rather than going to school with these stupid children," Evan said. "This voice... 'Are you blind?!' This is the same voice! He is the strange guy!!" Anita said. Evan confronted his crime. "Now would you tell us, why have you beaten all these children?" The police asked, "These stupid children! They have annoyed me, I try my best to avoid them, but they come to me, bully me and make fun!" Evan said. "What? But I never made fun of you, nor did Rain!" Anita said. "I was already annoyed by these children... Keith, Gloria, Louis. And you bumped on me twice, I got angry. I wanted to

satisfy myself, that's why I bet Daniel," Evan said. Then, he was prisoned for 1 and a half years.

About Evan Hendam:-

Born on 29th October 2004, a 17-year-old student, His quirks; Main- Can control rain and make raindrops into ice spikes (right now, can make only 1 ice spike at a time). Element; Water. Power Personality; Attacker. Got the quirk from his mother. Branch- Make anything made of air, it is also invisible (Right now, can make 3 things at a time.). Element; Air. Power personality; Tricker. Got the quirk from his father. Level, 3.2 Mid Tier. Has red eyes and brown hair.

"Man! Bullying can affect the children a lot," A cop said to the other, "Yeah, I agree!" The other one said. The victims went back to the school. After that day, there was no fighting, no one made each other's fun, and no one bullied each other. The high school was in a better place than before. Evan thought us a great lesson, but the way was not right. We should never bully others or make fun of them, it affects them a lot and makes them sad. Just like how Gregory was... "The strange guy's story is now over, but not mine!" Anita said.

CHAPTER XI

Everyone's life after high school

A year later, on 20th May, Anita's birthday. Anita was celebrating her birthday with her friends and parents. "Happy 19th birthday, Crete!" They said. Anita was happy, "But, where is Rain?" She asked. "Don't worry he will come, here is my gift" Anupma said and gave her the gift. "It's a beautiful dress, thank you!" Anita said. "And here is my gift," Mouny said. Everyone gave their gift. "Where the heck is Rain??" Anita said. "I am here!" Daniel said. "What took you so long?" Anita asked, "To prepare..." Daniel replied, "Prepare for what?" Anita asked. Daniel kneeled, and proposed to Anita, "Crete... we've known each other for a year. This year, I developed feelings for you. The day when I met you, I liked you. That's the only reason why I always blush seeing you, talking with you. Today, I got the chance, today I dare to tell you in front of everyone. Crete, I love you, so will you be my- girlfriend?" Daniel asked. Anita blushed and looked at her parents. "Please say yes!!" Mouny and Anupma said. "You know... I think Rain is a good guy, I think you should say yes" Anita's mother said. "Yes!! I will be!!" Anita said. Everyone celebrated. "YAY!!" All were happy. Everyone was happy. Now, everyone started to go to college, and coincidently, they met Keith in the same college. Daniel was happy seeing his best friend. "My bro!! You are here!!" Daniel said. A few weeks later, something unexpected happened. Keith proposed Mouny and she said yes. Keith liked her since high school... Everyone went to college happily.

The day came when Evan was out of jail. He didn't have any friends except Gregory... Evan called Gregory, "Hi, mate," Evan said, "Evan?? You are out of the jail??" Gregory asked, "Yeah... man. Can we meet? Somewhere, you decide" Evan said. "Let's meet at Winslain Park, here in the Super Town," Gregory said. "Okay," Evan said. Both went to Winslain Park, and met with each other... "Hi Greg," Evan said. "Hi, strange guy," Gregory said. And they started to talk. After a long talk, they went to their home. Somehow Evan got into the college where Gregory studies, and he met Gregory again, but this time, at his college. Gregory was shocked. And then, they became very good friends, and then, best friends. They always shared their sad and happy news with each other. A month later, Gregory met a nice girl in his class. Her name was Alice Marsh, "Hi Greg, you look so beautiful" Alice said. "Thanks? Your voice is also beautiful" Gregory replied. "Hmm... This guy has such a good face, if he becomes my boyfriend, I am pretty sure, everyone would be jealous of me!" Alice thoughtshe decides to take advantage of Gregory. Gregory liked Alice, he went to Evan and told him about this, "Man, I don't think Alice is a nice girl" Evan said, but Gregory didn't listen to him. "Greg! Being a good friend, I am warning you! I don't want you to make any mistake!" Evan said. But Gregory went away... A few weeks later, he proposed to Alice and as excepted, she said yes. Everyone started to be jealous of Alice, "Greg's girlfriend is Alice! She is so lucky" Everyone said. But, Evan wasn't happy seeing the couple. Gregory stopped talking with Evan, and Evan started feeling lonely... "My friend, when will you come?" He always asked himself. But, a few months later, Gregory and Alice's relationship wasn't so nice, and it became toxic! "Have you ever loved me? I never felt like that" Gregory said to Alice, "I do!" She lied. She never loved him. "You have to meet some of my friends, so be ready," Alice said. "Can't we just spend some time together instead of going and meeting 'your' friends?" Gregory said. But he had to go with her. He was not happy with all these, "Your boyfriend looks so handsome!" Her friends said. The couple always fought every day. And finally, Gregory understood that Alice was using him to show off others. "Evan was right! I did a mistake. Friends will never let you make the mistakes, he warned me but I was the one to ignore him, everything is my fault!" Gregory thought. The next day, Gregory called Alice, "What happened? Why did you call me?" Alice asked, "We need to talk! You are using me! When I met you, you were kind! But, now you are acting wild, impolite! I don't want to live with you. Your heart of ice, keep it to yourself, I don't need it! We are breaking up!" Gregory said, "I don't care! I never liked or loved you. You can go away" Alice said. And, Gregory went away angrily, he called Evan, "After 10 months, you remembered me?" Evan asked, "Yeah... I and Alice broke up, you were right! She used me" Gregory said, "I knew it" Evan replied. "So... I am sorry, I left you out alone" Gregory apologized, "It's okay, Wait, tomorrow is your birthday! We need to go buy a gift for you" Evan said, "Fine, let's meet at Winslain Park, then we will go to some mall, what do you think?" Gregory asked, "Okay for me, let's go!" Evan said. They met at Winslain Park, and then went to a mall and bought many things. The next day, Evan called Gregory at the Winslain Park, "Happy 20th birthday Greg!!" Evan said, Gregory was happy, "Thanks" He replied. "Here is your birthday cake!" Evan said and they both celebrated Gregory's birthday happily, "This is the best birthday of my life!!" Gregory said. "Evan, I have a question for you. Do you remember when Crete was trying to find you, she said your address is fake. If it is fake, then where do you live?" Gregory asked, "You don't know anything about me... Do you know Sky Town? My father has the royal bloodline and is the king of that town. So, being his son, I am the prince of Sky Town. I didn't want to show my real identity, so my parents made a fake address" Evan said. "WHAT!!!?? So!! My best friend is a prince!!" Gregory was shocked, "Yes!" Evan said and started laughing. "Evan, you know what? As I am having such a handsome face, I should use it in a good place instead of letting use it to someone else" Gregory said, "What do you mean, Greg?" Evan asked, "I mean... I should go to an acting school, learn acting and do movies, what do you think. I should be an actor!" Gregory said, "That's a great idea!" Evan said. After the small birthday party, both went to their house. The next day, Gregory told Evan, "I am going to the acting school!!" "Congrats bro!" Evan was happy for him. And, he started to go to the acting school for 3 years. But yet, Gregory always meets his best friend in the evening and tells him about the experience, "Today's day was so good! They said, my acting skills are very good" Gregory said. "I am sure, you are going to be a great actor!" Evan said, Gregory agreed. At the age of 23, Gregory did his debut in the movies. The first movie was 'Hiding move' and it was a hit! Gregory became a superstar in front of everyone, Evan was very proud of him... Gregory started to get many movies, "Evan, I am the lead role for 'The unknown girl!' I am the detective" He said to Evan, and Evan always smiles. "What about

you? When are you going to become the king?" Gregory asked, "At the age of 25, don't worry about me, take care of yourself. And remember, this fame can change you, but don't be. Just be how you are now" Evan advised. "I will never change!" Gregory said. He did many movies... From 'my revenge' to 'Sibling warrior', every director wanted to cast him. He became a famous actor. The day, when he went to promote his first movie. He saw the crowd, after many years. "This crowd... I was able to see it in the High school" Gregory thought. He saw a girl, screaming his name. Gregory went towards her, "Hi, what's your name?" He asked. "OMG!! Gregory sir!! I am your biggest fan!! Your acting in the movie was fire!! I love it!!" The girl said. It was the first time when someone complimented Gregory, not his face, but something else. Gregory was happy, he asked again, "What's your name?" "My name is Lily Sparks," Lily said. "You are very interesting, we should go out sometime," Gregory said, "Really, sir?? This evening?" Lily asked, "Sure" Gregory replied and went away. After the promotion, he told Evan about Lily, "I am going on a date with my fan, I am very excited!!" Gregory said. "I am sure, you two will be a good couple," Evan said. That evening, Gregory and Lily met, and talked with each other, they liked each other. A few weeks later, Gregory proposed to Lily, and she said yes! "What did you see in me, that you liked me?" Lily asked Gregory, one day. "Everyone... they see my face, compliment about it, and go away. But you saw my acting skills and complimented every scene, that shows how carefully you were watching the movie. I didn't see any other fan saying this" Gregory explained, Lily was happy hearing it. After 2 years of relationship, they decided to marry. They invited many people, their old friends, and also Evan! Gregory weds Lily. Everyone was happy with the marriage. Evan also became the king and maybe married also.

Meanwhile, Anita and Daniel married at the age of 24, after 5 years of relationship. They also called Gregory and Evan at the wedding. Keith and Mouny married at the age of 25, like Gregory. When Anupma was 22, she was a doctor and also had a flower shop, she worked in the hospital in the morning, and at the flower shop in the evening. As always, she was waiting for buyers to buy her flowers. Suddenly, a boy came to her shop, "Can I get a daisy?" He asked, Anupama gave her the Daisies. "Hey, what's your name?" The boy asked, "Anupma Reshan, you can call me Daisy" Anupma said. "My name is Gary Harmon, I am new here, so can you tell me where is the post office?" Gary asked, Anupma told him the way. The next day, Gary again came to the shop, "Hey, Daisy. Today I need some gnome plant..." He said, Anupma gave the gnome plant to him. "Daisy... I don't have any friends, I am very lonely here" Gary said. "I also feel lonely, my friends would be busy doing their jobs (Anita- Engineer, Daniel- Electrician, Mouny- Fashion Designer) "Ohh... Would you become my friend?" Gary asked. "Hmm... Sure, why not?" Anupma said. They talked every day... Gary worked as a software engineer and a gardener. They started liking each other. A year later, Anupma told Gary, "Gary, I think I like you" He said, "I also think" and took a Daisy bouquet and proposed to Anupma. And, of course, she said yes. And so, at the age of 25, after 2 years of relationship they married. Everyone lived happily ever after...

[THE END]

(spoiler!!!)

Characters and their name

Anita Hemishan- The protagonist, and wanted to know more about the strange guy

Darrel Powell- Owner of Duel and Duel Practice

Anupma Reshan- Friend of Anita

Daniel Wendon- Cousin of Anupma

Mouny Reshan- Cousin of Anupma

Keith Warner- Friend of Daniel and Mouny's husband

Shradha Howard Hemishan- Anita's mother

Harry Nash- Friend of Anita

Gregory Oak- Anita's schoolmate/ friend and the popular kid of the high school

Evan Hendam- The strange guy and best friend of Gregory

Alice Marsh- Gregory's ex-girlfriend

Lily Sparks- Gregory's biggest fan and his wife

Gary Harmon- Anupma's husband

Printed by Libri Plureos GmbH in Hamburg,
Germany